my kind of *perfect*

S.L. FORRESTER

Copyright © 2023 S.L.Forrester

All rights reserved. This book or any portion thereof may not be reproduced or used in any manner whatsoever without the express written permission of the publisher except for the use of brief quotations in a book review, or as permitted by U.S copyright law.

Independently published.

Please continue to support independent authors by obtaining their work from reputable sources, including online and physical bookstores. Let's work together in reducing the harm done to authors and readers by avoiding piracy and unofficial copies of authors' works.

This is a work of fiction. Names, characters, places, and incidents either are the product of the author's imagination or are used factiously. Any resemblance to actual persons, living or dead, businesses, companies, events, or locals is entirely coincidental.

Cover designer: CPR Designs

Contents

Dedication	IV
Prologue	V
1. Ash	1
2. Jace	13
3. Ash	22
4. Jace	30
5. Ash	39
6. Jace	43
Acknowledgments	49
About Author	50
Also By	51

To everyone that needed to see Jace as a dad

Prologue

Eight Months Earlier

Ash

Two pink lines appear on the test. I hang my head and try to breathe. How did this even happen, we weren't trying to get pregnant. I can trust Jace, he's not like that other piece of shit. *It's ok, in and out, in and out.* This time will be different because I won't settle for anything less. I'm older, much older, and I know what I deserve.

I toss the test on my bathroom counter with the other eight. I need to clear my head and think. Jace wants to meet me at the bar tonight when he gets off work but I can't drink now. I guess I will go ahead and tell him but I want to make it cute since this is his first pregnancy. *What could I do to make it unique? Hmmm. Maybe I could get something printed on a onesie... Oooh! I could get Silas to get a shirt too. His could say 'Dad's favorite soccer buddy.' The onesie could say 'Daddy's future soccer buddy'.* Yes! Now I am excited to do this. Jace's face is going to be a picture-perfect moment. I should call Izzy. Clara can take pictures. But first, I need to call Silas. I walk out of my bathroom, into my joint bedroom, and get my phone off the charger. I have one text message.

ASSHAT: I can't wait to see you. I miss you.

ME: You just saw me this morning while you were between my thighs.

ASSHAT: It was a delicious breakfast. 10/10 recommend.

I thought that after time Jace wouldn't want sex as often as he did when we first got together but boy was I wrong. That man fucks me every chance he gets. I didn't need an app to keep track of when we do it because we had sex every day, well except for the first couple of days that I was on my period. I leave the messages and pull up Silas's name.

"Hello."

"Hey, I need to tell you something and then ask a favor."

"Ok, what's up?"

"Don't say anything to Jace because it's a surprise."

"Ok."

"I'm pregnant. Do you think you can get your friend to make a couple of things for me?"

"Wow, ok cool. Yeah, I'll call her and see what I can get done. Just text me what you want."

"See if she can do it now because it will look weird when I get there and don't drink. I love you.

"I love you too, Mom."

Jace

Silas hangs up and slides his phone into his back pocket. He meets my eyes and he has this big ass smile.

"What the hell is wrong with you?" I ask, he just shakes his head and walks away. "Hey! Where are you going?"

"I have to go get something. The ring idea is great, go with that," he says and then he's gone, leaving me by myself in an almost empty bar. That was a little weird but whatever. Putting my focus back on what is in front of me -the ring- sitting there in its black velvet box. I'm staring at the simple tear-drop diamond sitting on top of a white gold band. Ash would have a fit if I gave her anything bigger than this. I've been holding on to this box for weeks, never feeling like it's the right time but tonight I'm going to shoot my shot. I really put thought into where to do it and the bar is the only place that makes sense. This is where we first met and hooked up, it's magical or whatever. I mean, we are basically married already, right? We live together and I even talked her into letting me try to put a baby in her. She still says no but I'm not like Silas's part-time dad. I actually give a shit and show her every day how much I love her. I want to prove to her every day that I want this and a baby, hoping she actually lets it happens. It took over a year but I proved myself enough to have her 'think about it'. That woman drives me crazy.

"So, what are you going to do?" The same fucking bartender works here.

"I think I'm going to put a toothpick through the ring and place it on top of a shot glass so that it's dangling," I enlighten him and he nods his head in approval. I don't fucking need it from him. Over the year that Ash and I have been together, he has made subtle passes at her.

I have to remind myself that she is in our bed at night, not his. Ash should be here soon, I wanted to do this before it got late and people started getting drunk. Where the hell did Silas go? He's supposed to be here for this. I decide to go ahead and order her drink.

"A shot of Jack and a toothpick, please," my voice harsh, just as I intended. He sits them down in front of me within seconds and I get it all set up, just in time because Ash is walking through the door now with Silas trailing her. I rub my sweaty palms on my jeans and try to slow my heart down before it jumps out of my chest. She is beautiful, wearing her white top, skinny blue jeans, and Vans. Her hair is down today which is surprising.

"Hey. Are you ok? You look flushed," Ash notices, shit. I pull her in for a hug and a quick kiss.

"Yeah, I'm all good. I love you so much, Ash," I start my proposal and then pause, looking at the shot glass. This makes her look at it too and she gasps. Her mouth drops and tears start to pool in her eyes. "I want to spend every fucking day with your smartass. I want the fights and all of the rough fucking. I'll even be okay with the regular sex too." Her hands shoot to cover her mouth and now she is full-on crying. This is the reaction I've only dreamed of. I get down on one knee. "Plus, Silas already said yes. Ash Rozanne Miller, will you marry me?" She hesitates and my heart drops. Her hands start fanning her face and I get to my feet.

"I'm sorry. Silas", she calls her son over and my hands start shaking with nerves. Shit. Silas walks up, I don't notice anything except Ash and the tears flowing down her face.

"Jace, I made this shirt to wear for you," Silas steals my attention and I try to pay attention. His shirt says 'Dad's favorite soccer buddy'.

"Yeah, I like it, man," I dismiss him.

"I have a present for you, Jace," Silas takes my attention again but this time he hands me a box. I drag my eyes away from Ash, to the box. I open it and it's a white onesie with the words "Daddy's future soccer buddy'. It takes a bit to process but once it hits, I drop the box and tears fill my eyes. My breathing picks up and my vision blurs. I bend to put my hands on my knees as I try to get myself together.

"Are we having a baby?" I ask her through the hoarseness of my voice. She nods her head fast and I jump up to hug her. It turns into picking her up and spinning her around. I place her back on her feet and take her face in my hands, kissing her between our pants.

"We are having a baby," she confirms for me.

"I am so happy, Ash. We are going to be great," I say to her.

"You are going to be an amazing father," she says through her tears. With all of this exciting news, I almost forgot that she hadn't answered my question. I turn to take the ring and bring it back to her.

"My question hasn't been answered," I remind her. She laughs and snatches the ring from my hand to put it on her finger.

"Yes, asshat. I thought that was obvious." Her smartass mouth is at it again but I'm too damn happy to care.

Chapter 1

Ash

Present Day

"I swear, Jace! If you keep pissing me off, I will kick you in the balls. You already knocked me up so I don't need them anymore", I scream at him. I'm eight months pregnant and I can't reach my shoes to tie them. Jace is standing there laughing at my attempts. He may be my husband now but still, fuck him. I'm sitting on the floor with my knee bent, trying my damnedest. After a few minutes, Jace decides to take his head out of his ass and help me. When my shoes are finally tied he stands up and walks out of the bedroom.

"JACE! I will divorce your ass," I yell at him. He comes back in with a shit-eating grin.

"I wasn't actually going to leave you down there." He sticks his hands in my face. "Come on, mama." That's his new nickname for me when it comes to anything evolving my struggle because of the planet that I'm carrying.

"It's not funny! This thing won't let me do anything," I cry out. He pulls me up and rubs my belly

"Hey now, that's my little girl in there," he says right before he bends down and kisses her. He has been picture-perfect, a complete 180 from my first experience. I was worried that he would put Silas on the back burner but he didn't. He always visits him at college and they talk on the phone every night. I am very blessed. Silas has already spoiled his sister. He has bought her so many stuffed animals and clothes. This girl has more shit than I do and she isn't even here yet! I know it's been a while for me but I feel like I kept Silas in plain-ass onesies.

I roll my eyes at Jace and walk out of the room.

"Come on, don't be like that." He stands behind me, wraps his arms around my hips, and nibbles my ear. After my morning sickness stopped, the sex drive zoomed up.

"Jace, everybody is outside waiting," I warn him but his hand slides into my stretchy yoga pants. Fuck, he knows I can't resist him. His other hand cups one of my breasts. They have gotten a little bigger since I got pregnant. I told him to play with them as much as he can now because I will start lactating soon. He doesn't pass up any opportunity. My head falls back to his shoulder.

"Fuck, Ash. I love how you are always so wet for me. Let me make you cum," he tempts. I moan and he takes that as the green light. He picks me up bridal style and lays me on our bed. I use to love it when he played with me while I stand but lately, my stomach is just too fucking heavy for that shit.

He pulls my pants down to my ankles and pops his head between my legs, my thighs resting on his shoulders. He doesn't tease or play around. His tongue is lapping my folds and it feels so fucking amazing.

"Damn, Jace. Hungry much?" I joke with him and his chuckle sends vibrations down my spine. Can this man get any sexier? He slides a finger in and slowly pulls out just to push back in. "More," I demand. This time when he pushes his finger in, another one is with it. "Faster," He speeds up and the wet slapping noise is bouncing off the walls. "Fuck, Jace. You're such a good fucking boy."

"Are you ready to cum for me?" He asks.

"Yes, yes, yes." I chant.

"Cum for me. Soak my fingers, show me how much you like it." He's so dirty with his words. But it s enough to send me over.

"Shit! Yes, Jace. Fuck, fuck, fuck. Don't you dare fucking stop," I yell as I claw at our sheets. My orgasms lately have been insane. I lay there for a minute to catch my breath. Jace helps me stand and pulls my pants back up. That was so good but my appetite isn't gone. I look down at his boner and bite my lip.

"Nope, we have guests," He's always the responsible one but I pout anyways.

"Please, I just want to suck it a little bit," I beg, knowing that I'm going to deep-throat him until I swallow every little bit of his salty cum.

"You don't know how to do anything with just a little. Let's go, we have a baby shower to host." He pulls me out of our room and I pout.

In our backyard, there are pink balloons everywhere. Hanging from trees, on the ground, and even getting tossed in the air between Silas and Clara. Jace set up a couple of patio heaters and it's keeping everybody warm. Of course, I have to have a baby in December when it's cold as balls. There's a long table with presents and a pretty pink sheet cake. As I get closer, I notice the cake has a white elephant drawn with icing. I try and keep my emotions in check but, well, it didn't happen. I ugly cried right there over the fucking cake. Luckily everybody is used to my shit, so nobody comes running. Jace hugs me from behind and lifts my belly a little to take away some weight.

"I'm sorry. These stupid fucking hormones! I'm so fucking tired of crying." I say between hiccups. Jace kisses the back of my head like the sweetheart he has been lately.

"There's nothing to be sorry for. This is a beautiful moment and you just happen to be the only person showing your emotions. Will it make you feel better if I start crying too? I'm sure I can muster up something."

"No, dumbass," I say and then I have this feeling that I am so tired of experiencing. "Shit, I have to pee, I'll be right back." I just fucking peed. I will not miss this part at all. I wobble my fat ass back into the house and to the bathroom. The struggle to pull my pants down and up is sad and embarrassing. After about five minutes in the bathroom, getting myself together, I slowly make my way back outside. Jace, Silas, Clara, and Izzy are playing cornhole. Melody and Hasley look like they are having a sexy conversation that I'm kind of jealous of. Don't get me wrong, the sex is so good but Jace is so concerned about the baby that he's gentle. I tried to choke him the other day and he told me no. He said that it would start something too rough. I get that I can't be tossed around but shit, pulling my hair won't hurt anything. Last week my leg hit the corner of my end table and I swear I almost came from the pain.

"Earth to Ash," Clara says, waving her hand in my face. I didn't notice that their game was over.

"Sorry, I spaced out. How are you doing?" I try to move the conversation off of me before I spill my thoughts.

"I'm good. Ready for you to open the presents! I've had to keep my gift a secret for far too long.' She's practically shaking with excitement.

"Well then, I guess I better do that now and then we can eat cake,' I walk towards the chair that has been set aside for me.

"Aren't you supposed to eat cake before presents?" She questions.

"I can do whatever I want. Plus, if I eat cake then I will have to drink something. That will only lead me back to the bathroom and the presents will never get opened," I explain to her as she helps me sit down. Melody and Hasley start bringing over the presents and I squeak with excitement. I love presents. Once all of the pink boxes and bags are at my feet, Jace gets to his knees and starts to give me them one by one.

I got a diaper genie, diapers, wipes, a shirt that says 'somebody's fine ass baby momma', cute little onesies, a bottle of Jack, a baby monitor, a white noise sound machine that looks like an elephant, and a milestone blanket. Somehow I ended up getting through all of it without crying.

"Hang on. I got something for you, Mom. Well, you too, Jace but don't really matter as much." Silas says and hands me a small bag.

"Look, I will be just as excited. Maybe even more, you never know." Jace picks with him.

"Remember that after you see what it is. I want waterworks." Silas looks so serious. I ignore them and pull out three white onesies. The first says 'My big brother is my hero', then there's one that says 'If you give me any trouble I'll tell my big brother', and the last one says 'I've got a crazy big brother and I'm not afraid to use him'. I'm already tearing up and then I pull out a picture frame. Damn, this boy. There's a handwritten note where the picture goes that says 'This is where me and my best friend will go'. The actual frame is wooden and says 'Ride or Die Besties'. Now I am full-on balling. I put everything back into the bag and give it to Jace, then pull Silas to me for a big hug.

"I love you so much, baby," I try to get out but it's all blubbery.

"I love you too, Mom. Can you let me go now?" He asks. I don't allow him to even budge.

"You did this to yourself, now accept it," I say as I get myself together. I hold him there for a little bit longer and let him go.

"Okay, Jace, I can't seem to find any tears," Silas calls him out. Their back-and-forths are usually funny. Sometimes it gets serious and I have to break them up.

"Fine, it didn't get me like it did your mom. But it's still pretty damn cute," Jace stands and pulls him in for a quick hug. It ended before it began and they moved on. It takes me a minute to pull myself together and I see the women crowding around Silas, showering him with kisses on his cheeks.

"Awe, you are the sweetest," Hasley says to him. I'm glad that Izzy found the two girls that make her happy, and oh is she happy. Every time I turn around, they are fucking. Like, out in public. There was that one time at my wedding, then in my backyard when they thought we were asleep -it was late at night-. But still, damn. I caught Silas watching them out the window. I had to get Jace to say something to him because it was too damn awkward for me.

"Can we do cake now? I'm hungry." Jace whispers in my ear.

"You just had something, but if you're still wanting more, I can give you something to eat," I wink at him and he bites his lip. He doesn't take me up on the offer and helps me up. He yells out for everybody to come get some cake and they are all there waiting on me by the time I make it. Of course, I'm already out of breath. Jace runs to get my chair and brings it to the table. I get comfortable and cut it into even squares. Well, I try but my cutting is shit. I take a small bite out of my piece and moan. It's vanilla with chocolate ganache.

"Damn, Ash. Do you need to change your pants? It's not nice to cum in front of everybody without letting us help." Izzy says and only part of me thinks she's joking.

"Can we not? I will leave, there are so many other things that I can be doing," Silas pipes up and says. Poor boy, he hears way too many conversations that he doesn't need to be a part of. It's not like he doesn't know about any of this, Jace has caught him.

They were still in his car… IN MY DRIVEWAY! I asked what he did when he saw them and Jace said he tapped on the window and handed him a condom. He assured me that it killed the mood and they stopped. We laughed a good bit until I realized they probably just drove somewhere to finish.

"Go ahead, Silas. We are done here anyways. Be good," I tell him and he gives me a kiss on the cheek and then runs off.

"Now that he's gone, how's the sex? I hear it's so much better when you're pregnant." Izzy asks and everybody turns to look at me. Except for Clara, who is fidgeting and looks very uncomfortable.

"You have no shame," I respond to Izzy. I don't want to make Clara feel any type of way. Just to get off of the topic completely, I grab some cake in my hand and throw it at Melody. She just misses it and her jaw dropped.

"Oh, girl. It's so on!" She yells in a playful way. The next thing I know, we are all throwing cake. Of course, it turns into Hasley licking it off of Izzy's face.

"Okay, okay, okay. Y'all are not fucking in my yard again. Now, hang out or whatever if you stop that, but I have to go pee again. I will probably fall asleep before I make it back out. So I want to thank everybody for coming to celebrate with us. The presents were very sweet," I tell them and give out hugs before I walk as fast as I can to the bathroom.

Exactly as I predicted, I sat on the couch and passed the fuck out. I woke up to Jace trying his best to pick me up to take me to bed but I'm just too big now. Sleeping, peeing, and eating is literally all I do. At least I'm not throwing up anymore. That first couple of months were ridiculous but Jace helped as much as he could. Held my hair back, rubbed my back, and just held me. I had so much peppermint tea then, that now I can't be near anything that smells like mint.

"Damnit, I tried not to wake you up. The couch isn't that comfortable for you to sleep on, you'll wake up to your back hurting." He stands in front of me, head down and hands on his hips. I try not to but I can't hold the tears back. "What did I say?"

"Nothing at all. You're just so amazing. I love you so much, asshat." I wipe the wetness off of my face and he helps me stand up.

"I love you too, my little smartass." He responds and kisses the top of my head. "Come on, let's go get a nap."

I love our king bed. It's a pillow top with a fluffy comforter. I wanted to have pretty decorative pillows but Jace said no. So he came home to twelve usable ones and he got the bright idea to stack a couple of them and lay me on top so that he has leverage to eat me out. I guess you could say that it was a win-win. Now that I'm super pregnant, I use almost all of them. One between my knees, ankles, behind my back, two under my head, one between my arms, and one under my belly. That being said, Jace has no room to cuddle me. I was going to get one of those body pillows but it's too bulky.

When I get to our room, he has it all set up for me.

"You are amazing," I tell him as I tear up... again. Fuck these hormones. I'm due in a couple of weeks and I can't fucking wait. Jace helps me up into the bed and pulls the blanket over my legs. I get too hot while I sleep so the blankets have to stay off of my arms. He kisses my head and I snuggle up to my pillows.

"Oh, don't forget the..." I start.

"Fan. I got you, babe." He winks before he flips the switch and walks out. It takes me just minutes to fall asleep.

"Welcome to the world baby girl." The doctor says as he hands my tiny baby to the nurse. She's so beautiful and I want to hold her but they don't let me. Why won't they give her to me? I want to scream at them but my voice isn't there.

"One down, one more to go." The doctor says as he stares between my legs. One more to go? What the fuck!

"Okay, Mrs. Baker, just like before. You are going to push while I count to ten, once I get to ten you can stop and take a breath." The doctor says. I'm so fucking confused. There was only one baby in there. Why am I still pushing? Jace is holding my hand with both of his and kissing my sweaty forehead.

"You are doing amazing, baby. Just a little bit more. You can do this. I love you." He chants in my ear. The nurse actually starts counting this time. She gets to nine and stretches the number out.

"Niiiiiiiiiiiinnnnnn..." She tries.

"Nine, ten. Done." I finish for her. Fuck this lady, thinking she's being cute or some shit.

"One more big push." The doctor directs me. I push down so hard that I know there's going to be a mess for somebody to clean up. A couple of minutes later I hear a little cry.

"You did it! I'm so proud of you." Jace says with tears running down his face. The doctor hands me both babies and I just stare at the little boy. I knew about the girl but where the fuck did this boy come from?

I wake in a panic. What the hell was that? I look down at my belly and poke it.

"There better only be one of you in there," I tell my little girl. Pushing the pillows off of me, I roll out of the bed and walk to the bathroom.

After I finish my business and wash my hands, I follow the wonderful smell of bacon. I love bacon, it's been my favorite food recently. Drench it in hot sauce and I'm in heaven. When I get to the kitchen, Jace is in his sweatpants that hang scandalously low and no shirt.

"Keep this up and I might let you put another baby in me," I say as I slap his ass.

"Is this all it takes? Feed you?" He asks with that smirk that I love so much.

"I was talking about the sex appeal. But food is a good runner-up," I tell him as I pick up a piece of bacon off of a plate. Time as I put it in my mouth, I melt. I have a dirty joke about that but I keep it to myself.

"Calm down, no need to cum." He jokes as he eats one with me.

"This would be the best orgasm I've had in a while," I shoot at him. Better to go ahead and have this conversation before sex is off the table after I go into labor.

Chapter 2

Jace

"I'm sorry, there's no way I heard that right," I tell her. I have made her cum so many times that I can't even count. I swear, if she says that she's been faking it, I'm going to question my entire life. She shoves another strip of bacon in her mouth and I want to pull it out but that won't lead to anything good. "Did you just say that I haven't made you cum in a while?

"No, that's not what I said." She muffles with her mouth full.

"Well, please fucking explain." I try my best to sound nice but this took me off guard.

"I said this would be the best orgasm that I've had in a while. You have been so gentle and sweet in bed lately. You won't hurt me or this baby. Maybe I just want you to bend me over, pull my hair, and fuck me like the good boy you are. Don't be scared to leave a handprint on my ass." My dick immediately gets hard after hearing that. I have been easy with her but that's not because I wanted to. Hell no, I just didn't want to hurt her. "Just fuck me, Jace." Time as that leaves her lips, I'm done. Games over I take her wrist in my hand and pull her to the kitchen table, spin her around so that she's facing it, hold her waist, and push her on her back so that she bends over.

"You want to be fucked, smartass?" It's rhetorical but she likes when I talk like this. She smiles but says nothing. I pull her pants down to her ankles and lick up her leg until I get to her ass, biting it. She still doesn't wear panties, it's nice but every once in a while, it would be hot if she did. I wrap her hair around my hand twice and pull, she lets out a yelp but continues to smile. I rub her clit for a minute and then run my finger to her entrance. "You're fucking soaked."

"Stop fucking playing around and fuck me already!" She yells at me. I pull her hair again and sink my cock into her. The best thing about her being pregnant is that I can feel all of her, raw. Nothing in the way. It took a couple of tries to last longer than a couple of minutes and it really pissed her off but now, I'm golden. I can last a good twenty minutes. I'm sure there are guys out there that can last longer but I'm damn proud of my almost half an hour.

She pushes her ass back to me, meeting my hips and I know she's really into this. I bring my hand down on her ass with a loud pop and I rub the sting out.

"No, I want to feel it. Let it burn," she says as she wiggles her ass on me. I slap the other cheek and let it stay. She screams out but doesn't push me away so I keep thrusting into her.

"Fuck, Jace. This is so good. The way your dick fills me up, fuck yes. Just like that." She moans and then her pussy clenches around me and she cums. Fuck, she feels so good.

"What am I?" I ask her, needing to hear it so that I can go over the edge.

"You're a good fucking boy." That's all she had to say. I grab her hips and my dick twitches as it spills inside of her. We stay just like that for a few minutes, trying to catch our breath. I ease out of her and she winces. I run and get a wet cloth to clean her up. She's still in the same position that I left her in, with a smile on her face. I wipe my cum off of her and pull her pants back up. She doesn't have to tell me what's next because I already know. She has to pee again and then lay back down. We are due in two weeks and I am so fucking excited. Ash is ready for it to be over with already but didn't want to get induced. She said she was not going to force labor like that unless it was a need, and it hasn't been.

"Hey, Ash," I yell out, there's been something that I've been wanting to get her but haven't had the chance.

"No, I will not pat you on the head and tell you that you did a good job." She thinks she's funny.

"Jokes on you, you already told me that while I was inside you." I hear her laugh as she walks out of the bathroom. "I have to go get something from the store, is there anything you want?"

"What store are you going to?" That means she does want something but doesn't want me to go out of the way.

"Whatever store has what you are craving." I have learned what to say and what not to say.

"Ice cream. The half-baked one from Jimmy Fallon." She has this sly smirk like she was already prepared and waiting on me to ask.

"I'll be right back, I love you." I give her a quick kiss and head to the baby store and then to the grocery store.

There are so many, which one is the best? I thought this would be a quick and easy trip. Damn if I was wrong. I'm staring at the breast pumps like I did when Ash sent me to get her tampons for the first time.

"It looks like you need some help. What exactly does she want?" A sales lady asks, I didn't even notice her walk up but was thankful nonetheless.

"Umm, she doesn't know that I'm here but I'm guessing something that extracts milk," I don't say that to be a smartass, I'm just so fucking lost.

"Good thing you found the pumps, it's what they do. Maybe I should narrow my question down a little. Does she want a manual one to where she has to squeeze the pump herself?" She asks and that just sounds exhausting.

"I don't think that sounds like something she's interested in. Is there one that can just plug in?" I ask and feel more stupid now than when I first walked in.

"Okay, is she going to want to walk around while pumping or would she rather stay sitting in the same spot?" Now that question makes me think a little harder. It would be nice for her to relax... but on the other hand, she doesn't like being restricted. "How about this, get this one." She hands a box with what looks like half globes in it. "She puts these in her bra, pushes the button and it pumps. No cords, very discreet, and the noise is minimal. Just have to remember to charge it when it's not in use." Damn, this is perfect. I thank her and go to check out. It's stupid expensive but so worth it. One less thing she has to stress about. Now on to get ice cream.

While I'm at the store, I call her to make sure she hasn't thought of anything else.

"Hey, is there anything else you can think of that you need?"
"Other than that dick, nope."
"Give me ten minutes, I love you."
"Tick-tock, I love you too."

We hang up and I run to get her ice cream and then decide to pick up flowers too. I use self-check-out because the lines are stupid and I don't have the time for that shit. I rush to the car but take my time driving home. We have a few rules and one of them is to never speed. Nothing is worth getting hurt over. When I make it home, Ash is sitting on the kitchen table... naked, pouring pancake syrup down her breasts. I drop the grocery bag and stride to her.

"I remember how much you enjoy the taste of syrup." She says and bites her bottom lip. I waste no time with small talk, my mouth is sucking on the swell of her breast. I lick my way down to her nipple and bite. Her head falls back as she moans, she fists my hair and pushes me to my knees. "Clean up the mess you made." I don't hesitate. My hands squeeze her thighs while my mouth suctions her clit. She slowly lays all the way down and I rise to my feet, bending over. My mouth hasn't left her, I wouldn't dare. My tongue slides down to her entrance and it pushes in. She tastes so fucking good, I'll never get enough. "Fuck, Jace. I need you." I keep licking and sucking. "Jace! Put your fucking dick inside me now! I want to feel you." It takes all of me to pull my mouth away from her but I do it. I pull my sweats down in one quick motion and thrust myself inside of her. Her legs wrap around me and I hold on to them so that she doesn't have to put any effort in. I'm squeezing her legs so hard that I know there will be a bruise tomorrow but she likes that shit. She gets heated every time she sees a mark on her or when she makes one on me. The positions are very limited with her due date being so close. As much as I love her being pregnant, I can't wait until I can turn her into a pretzel. She was so flexible.

"Oh shit, yes. Hang on, stop." She says and I pull out of her so fast.

"What's wrong? Did I hurt you?" I ask her, frantically. I knew I was being too rough, I should have slowed down.

"Nothing is wrong. Lay on the floor. I want to ride you." She has this sexy smile going on and I help her off of the table and then straddle me. I try to hold her waist but she slaps my hands away. "Put your hands over your head." She gets a little bossy sometimes which has been turning me on a lot. I do as she says and she starts bouncing on my dick. It doesn't take long before she gets tired and sits down completely. I almost move my hands to her but she gives me this 'I dare you' look, so I decide not to try my luck. She leans down, wraps her hand around my neck, and starts grinding on me. I try to think about anything else because I am about to cum and that's not allowed before her. Luckily for me, she's close. Her movements are getting frantic and the pressure on my neck is getting tighter.

"There you go, baby. Cum for me, let me feel that pussy squeeze my dick." When I start to talk, she starts convulsing. "Milk me, drain it all." I'm cumming with her and I swear it's the sexiest thing I get to experience. "Fuck yes, fuck, fuck, fuck." I fill her up and lay her down on her side. We stay like that for a minute and when I look over at her, she's falling asleep. I chuckle under my breath and get up to get a cloth. After I clean her, I pick her up and take her to bed. It is a little difficult but I'm not a pussy. Arranging all of the pillows the way that she likes them, she starts to smile in her sleep. I cover her up and turn the fan on before walking out of the door. She's going to need a bath when she wakes up because she's still really sticky. Which reminds me that there's ice cream that is currently melting on the floor. Shit. Maybe it's not that bad and I can just put it in the freezer. She's going to notice, that woman sees everything. It's a little creepy sometimes. It's fine though, melted for sure but the plastic around the top kept everything inside. It'll freeze back, and won't be as good but it will be fine. She'll eat it all the same. Now for the flowers. I'm way overdue for changing them out but Ash hasn't once complained. I throw away the very dead ones and wash the vase out. I pour clean water in, flower food, and then cut them to the proper size. Oh, I have learned. As I'm putting the flowers in, Ash screams. I drop everything and run to her, she's sitting on the edge of the bed holding her stomach.

"What's wrong? Is she ready?" I'm panicking at this point. She grabs my hand and squeezes.

"I think it's time." That's all she has to say and I'm putting a dress on her. We slowly get to the car and I take off.

"It's okay, baby. We are almost there, you're doing great. Remember to breathe in and out, just like the doctor showed you." We are right around the corner and she starts to calm down. I park and help her out of the car. When we get to the automatic doors, I yell out for a wheelchair and go straight to the Labor and Delivery floor. It only takes a minute to get checked in and into a room.

"I'm okay now. Maybe it was nothing and I just overreacted. It is a couple of weeks early." She starts to tell me but I'm not letting her talk like that.

"Even if she's not ready, this is a perfect test run. I'm happy no matter what." While I'm trying to soothe her, the nurse is hooking up two monitors on Ash's stomach.

"These will record the baby's heartbeat and your contractions. Just lie back and try to relax, the doctor will be in soon." The nurse tells her and leaves. We stay quiet and watch our baby's heartbeat on the monitor. It's beautiful and I can't believe how lucky I am. After a few minutes, the doctor walks in and makes small talk while looking at the printout papers of her contractions.

"How are you feeling?" He asks Ash.

"Silly. I didn't have any contractions since I've been here." She tells him.

"Hey, don't say that. I would rather be here and nothing happen than be home and have to play football. Soccer is my sport so I have no interest in catching her when she pops out." I kiss the back of her hand and the doctor interrupts.

Chapter 3
Ash

Braxton Hicks. I should have known that. It's not like this is my first kid, I know better. Granted, I had Silas a while ago but still. I feel stupid when we get home so I go straight to the bathroom and start a bath. No, you're not supposed to take one this late in pregnancy but fuck it. Jace tried to join me but I waved him off. I need time to myself but I do hear him on the phone in our bedroom. It's muffled so it might just be the T.V. but whatever. I don't really care at this point. I got so excited, thinking that it was time and I was going to come home with my baby girl in my arms. This is so annoying but that's what I get for trying to rush it.

The hot water feels amazing and it's just what I need. Ooo, some food would be good too.

"Jace!" I yell and he comes rushing in. Okay, maybe I shouldn't have been that loud because he looks scared as hell. I can't help but laugh.

"What's wrong?" He asks after studying me.

"Can you bring me a little snacky snack, please?" I ask with a big, cheesy smile. He just rolls his eyes and walks out. I'm thinking that he has had enough of my shit but then he comes back in with leftover Chinese. My mouth waters when the smell hits my nose.

"Damn girl, if you want my dick that bad all you have to do is ask, don't drool over it." He thinks he's so funny but that does give me an idea.

"Come here and stop playing," I order him and he does as he's told. I get to my knees and reach out for his sweatpants, pull them down and his dick pops out. There's a bead of precum at his tip so I lean in and lick it off while holding eye contact. He loves it when I look up at him while I take him in my mouth. I lick his tip again and then up his shaft, then I suck on his balls for a minute.

"Fuck, Ash. Why are you teasing me?" He asks between his teeth.

"Because it's so much fun to watch you squirm," I say right before I wrap my lips around the head. He grunts and I give in. I grab his ass with both hands and pull him further into my mouth. I pull him out and spit on his length, rubbing it all in so that it's all wet and slippery. Then continue bobbing while stroking the little bit that doesn't fit. His hands tangle in my hair but he knows not to push. I will gag on him when I'm ready, I don't like to be forced.

"Shit, you're so good at this. The way you're tongue licks while you suck, fuck." He moans and that makes me take him deeper while I play with his balls. He starts to shake and tugs my hair back. "I'm about to cum.' I pop him out of my mouth and stare.

"Let me swallow you." I don't smile and then suck him to the back of my throat. His salty warmth hits and I take every little bit. After he finishes, I lick his shaft and the tip to make sure I get it all. I look up at him and smile. "Can I have my food now? I am actually really hungry." He laughs but hands the container over. Brown rice with sesame chicken and shrimp. He also brought me a cup of sweet tea. "I love you."

"I love you too... almost as much as I love that mouth." He jokes and I splash him, soaking the floor more than him.

"Asshat." I laugh and he leaves me to my happiness. He won't dare say anything to me about this. He tried once and I will admit, I got a little violent. Showed his ass.

The two weeks went by slow. Jace wouldn't let me do anything and Clara kept telling me that the coffee shop was running perfectly. I know she's lying. It's not possible for a business to be perfect for weeks at a time. Something has to be fucked up but I guess I won't know for a while. I'm the fucking owner, why can't she just tell me. My phone starts ringing and I'm so happy for the distraction.

"Hey, baby."

"Hey, Mom. Pop her out yet?"

"Nope. What have you been up to? I feel like we don't talk much anymore."

"I was just at the baby shower. We talked there."

"That was two weeks ago and you know that's not what I mean."

"I've just been trying to get everything ready to start school. There's a lot that I need."

"I'm so proud of you. College is going to be so much fun. What do you need? You know I'm going to help you with your books but what else?"

"Sports medicine doesn't really need much."

"Fine, but when you think of something, tell me."

"Okay, Mom. I just wanted to see if I have a sister yet since you're due today."

"Nope, she must be more stubborn than you. Fun."

"I think it's genetics. I'll talk to you a little bit later, I love you."

"Haha, you're so funny. Not really. I love you too, deep down."

We hang up and I go back to bouncing on my yoga ball. I'm all about keeping her in there to cook more but damn, it's time.

"What do I need to do to get you out?" I think I've asked my belly this at least twelve times a day for the past week.

"We can always have more sex. I'll take one for the team." Jace scares me when he walked into our room. I thought he was at work and he didn't call me.

"What the fuck, Jace. You scared the shit out of me." I throw my hand on my chest and try to steady my breathing.

"Apparently that's the only thing that I scared out because I still don't see a baby." He thinks he's so funny.

"You mean she's still in there? I had no idea." I roll my eyes at him. I've been extra bitchy lately and it's not fair but I can't help it. He comes up to me and starts kissing my neck and nibbling on my ear. And that's all it takes for me to be turned on.

"You know, I hear there are things that I can do to help the process." He whispers in my ear and I shiver.

"Oh yeah? What kind of things do you have in mind?" His hand runs down my side, around my thigh, and cups my pussy. He slowly starts rubbing me and my head falls back to his shoulder. Suddenly his hand stops and my eyes pop open.

"Excuse me?" I allow my attitude to show and he has the audacity to smile.

"If you stay on this ball then it will end badly." Okay, he has a point. I let him help me up and take me to the bed. It seems like the bed is the only place that this can happen lately, everywhere else is just uncomfortable. I lay down and he takes my pants off. In no time at all, his tongue is lapping at my clit. I want to twist my fingers in his hair but my stomach is too big and I can't reach. His fingers are digging into my thighs and that has me squirming with need. He penetrates me with his tongue and that feeling is like no other. It's a simple move but there's something about it that makes me feel dirty.

"Fuck, Jace. I'm about to…" I almost finish but somebody's phone starts ringing. Jace stops for less than a minute to think and decides it's not important. He thrusts two fingers into me as he sucks on my sweet spot. I cum but it's not as hard as it usually is. The phone must have messed with my head. "I swear whoever called better have had something important to say. New rule... no phones in the room when it's sexy time." He stands and has this sorry expression on his face. I just lay there for another few minutes while he checks to see what was so important.

"It was just Izzy. She sent a text after I didn't answer." He smiles and shakes his head while he types out a response to her.

"Well, are you going to share with the class?" I say it more in a joking tone.

"She said that if I could fuck you the right way and stop being a pansy, then her niece would be out already."

"I guess you better work on that then. Maybe she will give you some pointers, she is keeping two women around." That statement would have been better if I wasn't struggling to sit up. It takes away from the badassery that I was going for.

Jace pushes me back down and hovers over me.

"I apologize, let me fix this for you." He whispers in my ear and stands to his feet. His hands wrap around my ankles and pulls me to the edge of the bed. I let out a little squeal and his smile makes me incredibly happy. He leans down and starts sucking and nipping at my neck. My breasts have been off-limits lately because they are so ready to feed the baby. I'm into some kinky shit but breast milk isn't my thing. Not saying anything is wrong with it, it's just not for me.

He helps me stand and then twists me to face the bed. I thought he was going to do something sweet but then he pushes me to bend over and slaps my ass hard. My hands fall to the bed and he taps my thighs to get me to spread them. His fingers slide between my folds and my back arches. I hum out an approval and his hand moves away. The cold air brushes my wetness and I shiver. Before I can look back to see what he is doing, his dick is filling me. It stung for a second but the pain went away after he started pumping in and out.

"Fuck, that feels so good," I moan through clenched teeth. He bends over me so that his chest is on my back, then nibbles on my ear.

"Am I fucking you right? Or do you still think that I need some training?" He snarls.

"Holy shit, yes," I scream as he stands back up and pulls my hair by the roots. He has never been this rough before. I'm not sure if I like it for an all-the-time thing but for now, this is okay. "AHHH, Jace! I ... I ..." The sentence ends there with another scream. Chills run down my spine, toes curled, fingers gripping the bedsheets for dear life. My orgasm hits and fuck, it takes over. I don't feel Jace cum but I know he did when he helps me lay back down. He leaves and comes back with a wet cloth.

"Are you okay? You kinda had me scared at the end there." He asks as he cleans me up. I am still calming my heart but I nod. Words aren't a thing at the moment. I sit up and he hands me a cup of water, I gulp it down like I haven't had any in months. It takes me a second to get my bearings together. Jace is staring at me like I'm about to break.

"What?"

"You just seem a little different. I'm waiting for you to say something... anything." He tells me like it's obvious.

"I'm fine, it's just never been like that with us before. But not in a bad way at all. I do have to pee pretty badly though." I assure him as I get up, kiss his head, and head to the bathroom. Of course, he follows.

"Are you sure?"

"Jace! Yes, everything is good. Stop worrying." I laugh as I say it. This man is too much sometimes.

"Is she popping out yet?" I swear if he asks about labor one more time.

"Yup, I see a head and everything... No! You would know if it was time." I fuss and he walks off. I don't mean to come off this way all of the time but sometimes his brain doesn't work. Now I feel like shit so I go to bed and cuddle up to him. "I know you are excited, I am too. I promise when it's time, I will make it very clear. I promise "

"I love you and I can't wait to meet her." He rubs my stomach and she kicks him. It's rare that he actually felt it. Most of the time, she stops time as his hand touches me. The way his eyes light up makes me tear up.

"She loves you too." I drift off to sleep while he talks to her, I can't help it.

Chapter 4
Jace

Two weeks.

Two weeks of fucking Ash as much as possible.

Two weeks of doing everything we can to put Ash in labor.

Two weeks past my baby's due date.

"Good morning, Iz." She's always waiting for me at work. Until my baby is born, I have to work. Unfortunately, the water and electric company doesn't care what's happening. I still need to pay them.

"How does it look?" Izzy asks me the same thing every single day. And when I don't work, she texts.

"I'm doing fantastic, thank you for asking." I smile but she isn't having it.

"I give no shits about you." She punches me in the arm and it actually does hurt a little.

"I don't know, Iz. I can't tell and she is just irritated. You are on the call list when things start happening." That list is only her and Silas. So not really a list.

"Hey, Jace. I get you another day?" One of my trainees asks.

"Yeah, man. I can't promise any other day but you have me for now." I stretch my arms out, gesturing to me.

"Good. I'm a little scared of Ms. Izzy." He says in a low tone but she still hears him and rolls her eyes.

"Oh, Jace. Just wanted to let you know that Melody inked Silas last night." She drops that on me and it takes me by surprise.

"It wasn't something stupid, right? Was it small?" I start spitting questions at her.

"Uh, yeah, sure." She says but the big ass smile on her face says otherwise.

"So, I'm just going to go over there and stretch out a bit." My trainee says and almost runs away. Good choice.

Izzy skips - yes, skips - to the other side of the front counter.

"Iz..." I give her a minute to make me feel better but her smile just gets bigger.

"It's nothing bad. I promised him that I wouldn't tell you about one small part of it but he got half of a sleeve. And some on his chest. Most of it is just lines and I approved." That calms me a little. Ash is going to flip her shit when she sees him. Fuck, I hope it's not something stupid. That kid is going to drive me crazy. Izzy just stands there smiling. Whatever, I have to start working.

The man is doing toe touches when I finally get to him. He doesn't ask questions about the conversation that took place in front of him. That's good because I'm in an oddly bad mood today. I think I'm just getting impatient with this baby's arrival. If she doesn't make her appearance soon, Ash is going to have to have the labor forced. Fourty-Two weeks is long enough. I bring my mind back to work and the day goes by pretty fast.

After I finish up my shift, I call to check up on Ash, and then I do my own workout. I like to keep up with my body, keep myself toned and defined. It makes me feel good about myself and Ash gets wet over it. Win-Win. I throw in my earphones and drown in the music.

When I make it home, Ash is on the couch sleeping with a box of pizza on the table beside her. Damn, I'm lucky. I'll take her to bed after I get a shower, I can smell myself so I know she will have a problem with it. I head to the bathroom and strip down, turn the water on, and wait for it to warm up. Normally I would start the shower first so that I don't have to stand here naked and stupid but those clothes were nasty and sticking to me. Luckily it doesn't take long for it to hit the perfect temperature. I'm not one for long showers but I take my time with this one. I haven't touched myself since I got with Ash, haven't needed to. After I get clean, I think about stroking it a little but decided not to. I'll give the man a break, he's been working a lot lately. I turn the shower off, step out, and freeze. We are getting close to mid-December and it is so cold. We are too south for snow but it does ice up outside, which reminds me that I need to let the faucet drip so that the pipes don't freeze. I dry off quickly and go into my closet for a shirt. When I step into our bedroom, Ash is sitting on the bed, naked. So glad I didn't fuck my hand.

"I thought you were asleep?" I ask her the stupidest question. She was obviously sleeping.

"I had a dirty dream and woke up wet. Just wondering if you would like to fix this problem for me or if you are going to drive me mad." She's always wet for me but I have no intention of ever turning her down. I don't respond and hop onto the bed, throw her legs over my shoulders, and dive in. She immediately starts moaning. I've learned all of her spots and what her movements mean. It's a science, really. I take my time with her though. She doesn't need to cum just yet. I lick around everywhere but that spot that sends her over, teasing her.

"Jace, make me cum. I want to." She begs me but I don't let it happen.

"I want you cuming on my dick." I get to my knees, wrap my hands around my shaft, and slap it on her pussy a couple of times. This makes her eyes roll back and she lets out a frustrated noise. Deciding she's waited long enough, I slowly slide inside of her. She tightens around me and cums, loudly. I pump into her a couple more times but stop when something feels off. Pulling out, liquid comes with me.

"Ash, you're really wet." Normally it's a good thing but this is different.

"If I wasn't then you wouldn't be doing it right." She's not understanding. Does she not feel all of this?

"No, like seriously wet." She sees the seriousness on my face and sits up as fast as she can to look at the sheets. I look back up to her face and she's crying.

"Jace! That's my water, you asshat!" She yells at me and I freak out.

Oh my God! This is it, she's going to pop. What do I do? Am I supposed to call somebody? No, get the bag! I get off of the bed and trip over my own feet, jump up and run to get the hospital bag. Throwing it over my shoulder, I run back to Ash. She's trying to put her leg into her pants.

"Ash, we need to hurry before she falls out!" I'm over here rushing and she starts laughing. I help her into her pants and drag her out of the bedroom door.

"Look, I'm all for loving yourself but maybe you should worry about putting your own clothes on. Yeah? I wouldn't want your dick to shrivel up into your body." Oh shit, I forgot that I am butt-ass naked. I drop the bag and throw on some sweats and a shirt. "Socks?" Fuck. My brain is running faster than it should. I'm supposed to be the calm one and she's supposed to be freaking out. While I'm putting my socks on, she walks out of the room and laughs. I'm glad she thinks this is funny. I run and catch up with her.

"How are you so calm right now?"

"I've done this before, remember? Also, I'm not even having contractions yet. Calm down, it's okay." She tries to soothe me but I can't stop flipping out. I grab my keys, wallet, and phone. I rush her out of the door and help her into the car. I didn't notice the towel in her hands until she places it on the seat before sitting. I try not to speed to the hospital but I end up doing it anyways. Luckily, the roads are close to empty so we get there in no time. Parking on the other hand, yeah, it's a bitch. I don't want her to have to walk far so I park at the entrance and walk her in. I tell the front desk lady what's going on and she brings Ash a wheelchair.

"I'll be right back, just going to go park. Don't have my daughter without me." I tell her and rush out to the car. I drive around and finally find a spot, grab the bag, and run back inside. Ash is exactly where I left her but there's a nurse behind her, waiting for me.

"Alright, let's go have a baby," Ash says with a big smile. I give her a quick kiss and I follow them into the elevator.

"Is this your first?" The nurse asks.

"My first but this will be her second." I respond and Ash gives me this 'shut the fuck up' look.

"My son is seventeen so I'm not baby daddy hopping or anything." She says defensively.

"Oh no, I wasn't thinking that at all. That's a big age difference but I'm sure the big brother is excited." The nurse says.

"He has already spoiled her, so I am scared to see how much he gets when she's actually here." I jump in and say. Luckily we reach our floor and the awkward conversation can end. When the doors opened, we were guided to the nurse's station to get some paperwork out of the way. It didn't take too long to finish up and be taken to a room. I walk in behind Ash and stop dead in my tracks. This room is huge, definitely bigger than any hospital room that I've stayed in.

"Are you planning to stay in the doorway or did you want to be a part of this?" Ash asks, taking me out of my daze. The nurse is giving her a gown and saying something to her but I can't hear anything. Everything is getting so real and it all hits me. *We are having a baby.* I bend over and my hands fall to my knees. I feel my breathing pick up and my heart is pumping out of my chest. I don't realize the nurse beside me until she's leading me to a chair.

"Mr. Baker, you're having a panic attack. I need you to concentrate on your breathing. Take a deep breath in and hold, hold, hold... Now let it out slowly." I do as the nurse tells me and I start to feel better.

"You do know that I'm the one in labor right now, right? I'm supposed to be freaking out... not you." Ash is staring at me with concern all over her face. "Come here." I move over to her and she grabs my head to pull me in for a kiss. "It's okay to be nervous but remember, we want this. You are going to be a perfect dad and she is going to love you."

"I know, I'm sorry. We can do this. I love you." I kiss the top of her head and breathe her in. She grabs my hand and squeezes hard. It has me falling to my knees. "Hey, what's wrong?" I start to panic again and her face is scrunched up like she's in a lot of pain. I place my other hand on her stomach and it is rock hard. "I'll go get the nurse."

"No, just... hang on." She says through gritted teeth. I don't know how to help her so I pet her hair and tell her how she's doing an amazing job. There's a knock on the door and the same nurse comes in, reads the room, and rushes over.

"How long has the contraction been happening?" She asks and I take a second to think about it.

"Maybe two minutes." I give her my best guess and she writes something down in her notepad. At this point, Ash's grip loosens and the blood starts to flow through my hand again.

"Okay, I'm good now. Yeah, that hurt." Ash says and the nurse tells her to change into the gown before another contraction starts, then she leaves.

"I'm so sorry that you have to go through this. I wish I could make this better." I feel so useless right now.

"It's worth it in the end. Just help me get changed." She starts to slide off of the bed and I help her stand and take her clothes off. Before putting on the plain, light blue hospital gown, I kiss her stomach and tell my daughter to take it easy on her mom. After everything is on and tied, I help her back into the bed and press the call button for the nurse. It takes almost no time before she comes barging into the room.

"Okay, Mrs. Baker. Let's set you up to all of the monitors and start your IV." She wraps the two devices over her stomach like the ones from before. The needle goes into Ash's hand with no problem and I wince. I don't know how she's so calm with it in her hand. I'm good with the arm but my hand... nope. I'm going to pass. After everything is said and done, the nurse says that the doctor will be in soon to check her cervix.

"You have had so many fingers inside of you lately. Should I be worried?" Joking, obviously but somebody needs to lighten the mood.

"Completely. I'm really thinking about taking my doctor home with me. The way he stabs my cervix over and over again... mmm, I'm getting wet just thinking about it." She burst out laughing and then immediately stops when another contraction starts.

Chapter 5

Ash

I have been in labor for three hours and the contractions have been back-to-back now and I'm regretting passing up the epidural. Fuck this hurts. Jace has been trying to help as much as he can but there's really nothing he can do. He has been running back and forth to keep my cup full of ice chips, wiping my head with a wet cloth, and telling me how amazing I am. The doctor walks in towards the end of a contraction and patiently waits for it to pass before he starts talking. I may or may not have snapped the last time he was in here. There's no point in talking when I'm in pain. I won't be listening so he was basically talking to himself.

"Ash, since your contractions have been so close together, I'm going to check to see if you've dilated anymore." He tells me as he pulls on gloves and motions for me to slide down to the edge of the bed. If anybody thought this was sexual, they are so very wrong because his fingers fucking hurt and the whole thing is uncomfortable.

"Almost there. You are at nine centimeters. I'll have a nurse stay in here with you but I'm going to say we will be pushing very soon." The doctor says, throwing his gloves in the trash before walking out of the door.

"Ash, we are having a baby. We are finally going to be able to hold our daughter." Jace's eyes start to get glassy but then he wipes his face to remove the evidence. "I'm going to call Silas and Izzy to tell them that they can make their way up here."

"Okay but make it..." Another contraction hits me and fuck, why did I get pregnant again?

It's worth it, it's worth it, it's worth it.

I have to chant to myself over and over again. The nurse is at my side holding my hand and telling me that it won't be much longer. I breathe through the pain and bring myself back to where I am.

"I know he just looked but I would like to check you." The nurse says and I lay back, spread my legs and yet another stranger gets to look at my goodies. After a while, it doesn't matter anymore. I look over to see Jace still talking on the phone. I'm actually pretty surprised that he hasn't rushed over here. The nurse doesn't even touch me before she runs out of the door. That catches Jace's attention and he hangs up.

"What's wrong? What happened?" He asks while my legs are still wide open. He takes a look down there and his eyes bug out. "There's a whole ass head."

The doctor and three nurses barge into the room and they have on gowns and face shields. It is actually a bit scary.

"Ash, are you ready to have a baby?" The doctor asks with an excited face. Jace starts kissing my head and my hand. The doctor put on his gloves and started feeling around.

A stabbing pain starts in my stomach and stretches down to my hips. It is unbearable and I want it to stop. The doctor tells me to push and Jace is in my ear telling me how much he loves me and how beautiful I am. I want to be nice but I hurt so intensely that I can't.

"Stop lying! I look like shit and you did this to me! You and that stupid dick just had to fuck me up!" I yell at him while continuing to push. The nurse is on my other side holding my leg all the way to my head.

"Okay, take a few seconds to breathe." The doctor says and then whispers something to the nurse.

"You're doing so great, Ash. You are almost done, just a little longer and we can hold our daughter." Jace tells me as he smoothes out my hair. I'm about to respond but the doctor tells me to push again. I try so hard but it feels like my hips are being ripped apart. There's no way my vagina is going to look good after this. I was smart when I had Silas, epidural all the way. This shit is for the birds.

I pushed for another three more rounds and stopped once I heard that sweet cry. Everything around me stopped as I watch the perfect little girl get passed from the doctor to the nurse. She sucks everything out of the baby's nose and mouth and then lays her on my chest. Tears start falling from my eyes and I am so happy that I can't feel anything but the love that I have for this little girl. After a few minutes, the nurse takes her from me to check her weight and heartbeat. I'm sure there's more but my focus goes to Jace, who is pulling my face to his for a kiss.

"You are so fucking perfect." He whispers when he pulls away.

"I know," I agree with him and his smile widens.

"Such a smartass." We are interrupted by the nurse when she hands the baby back to me but this time she is wrapped up in a blanket. She needs to eat, so I pull my boob out and place my nipple in her mouth. It takes her a minute to figure it out, but when she does, she sucks the milk down until she is fast asleep. I had all of my attention on her that I didn't notice the room clear out. Jace has also been strangely quiet. I look up to him and he has his phone out taking pictures. I gesture for him to take her and spend some much-deserved time. When he does, I start crying again. This is perfect and I couldn't ask for anything more. I ask him for his phone and then I start taking the pictures.

Chapter 6

Jace

"Ivy Lee Baker, you are perfect. My little princess, you will get everything you want and we won't tell your mom. She's a buzzkill and will tell you no." I look up to see Ash sleeping and I can't help to think that this is my kind of perfect. I have the most amazing wife, the sweetest stepson, and now an angel of a daughter. Can it be any better? Hell no.

Ivy coos and stares at me. I know she can't see me but I'm hoping she recognizes my voice from all the talks we had while she was swimming around. She has blue eyes and a small amount of dark hair. The nurse said she is seven pounds and twenty inches long. Perfect.

There's a knock on the door and Silas walks in. He looks so excited when he sees Ivy that he is almost jumping up and down.

"Can I hold her?" He asks and I tell him to sanitize his hands first. When I hand her over to him, his face lights up even more and I love it. "She looks just like you and Mom. I thought that she was going to wait until Christmas."

"Look, December the eighteenth is close enough. I don't know if I would be able to handle it if it was any closer. So…

Izzy told me you got a tattoo." I was going to wait until he came out with it but I have no patience.

"Yeah, but I want to wait until Mom wakes up. It's special, well a piece of it is." That doesn't help my anxiety at all.

"Okay, well how is school going?" I try to start up a conversation that will take my mind off of the ink.

"I decided to take a little break and start back next year." He takes me off guard with that one because he usually tells me everything that happens in his life.

"What happened?"

"I just want a little break. Plus, the girl that broke up with me was in all of my classes and I can't be around her. It hurts." He explains and then goes back to talking to Ivy. I knew a girl broke up with him but I had no idea it was such a serious relationship. I don't want to nag him so I drop it for now. Just in time too because Ash starts to stir.

"Silas! I'm glad you're here. I've missed you." Ash says and Silas hands Ivy back to me. She is now fast asleep and I swear she is the perfect baby. Silas gives his mom a hug and tells her that he wants to show her something. She sits up rather quickly and I walk around to her other side to lay Ivy down in her crib. Silas pulls his navy shirt over his head and there it is... tattoos covering the top half of his arm, shoulder, and his right peck. He has a soccer ball, an actual heart, a stethoscope, the symbol of Caduceus, and a bunch of lines that tie it all together. Across his chest is the name 'Ivy' with more lines to fill in the blanks. Ash is bawling her eyes out and I can't stop staring at it.

"What do you think?" Silas asks after a while of nobody talking.

"It's beautiful, baby. I can't believe you did this, I love it. Come here." Ash waves Silas over to her and pulls him in for a long hug.

"Okay, Mom. Very sweet, got it. Can you let me go now?" Silas tries to pull away but gives up. When Ash isn't done holding you, you won't be able to get away. Ivy starts to make noise and Ash drops her hands to look over to check on her. I decide to stay back and let them have their mother-son thing. There will be plenty of time for me to hover. Silas picks his sister up and hands her over to their mom.

"Daddy, somebody needs a diaper change." Ash has this baby-talk tone in her voice.

"Alright, Silas lay down, and let's get this over with." I try to joke with him but apparently, he is very confident in himself and starts to go for his jean button.

"Let's go, man." He jokes back and I miss this. I miss our back-and-forth banter.

"Yeah, maybe go find somebody else to take care of that for you." I pull out the diaper and wipes that the hospital supplies and change Ivy. She has on a zip-up onesie with the footies so I play with her tiny toes before tucking them back away. When I pick her up and hold her close to my chest, she moves her face from side to side with a wide open mouth.

"Sorry princess but I don't have anything for you." I hand her over to Ash and Silas goes to sit down and bury his face in his phone. "At least somebody gets to give them attention." I wine to Ivy but she doesn't care because she is going to town on her snack. "Do you want anything? Chips, soda?" I ask Ash as I head to the door. I need something to drink and to move around.

"Yes please, just surprise me." She responds and I walk out and head to the elevator.

When I get back to the room, Ash is on a video call showing off Ivy.

"That is a bomb ass baby! Look at her, she's fucking amazing." I hear Izzy say over the speaker and decide not to join in on that conversation. Instead, I go into the bathroom to relieve myself.

Ivy has been home for one week and I'm going crazy.

"What is wrong? Why will you not stop crying?" I ask Ivy like she's actually going to answer. Ash is taking a shower and Ivy has not stopped since she was handed over. She was just fed, I changed her diaper, and I don't feel like she could possibly be sleepy. Ash walks into the living room with us and I'm breaking down. "I don't know what I'm doing wrong. I've changed her, bounced with her, and rocked her. Why will she not stop?" I'm having a whole-ass meltdown. Ash just smiles and rubs my back.

"Y'all just need to find out what y'all have in common. You will figure it out and when you do, it will be amazing. You are a great dad, just find your groove." She is the most encouraging person and if it wasn't for a crazy baby in my arms, I would kiss every part of her body. "I'm going to the store but I will be right back. I love you." She kisses me and then leans in to kiss Ivy on her head. "Y'all are going to be great." And just like that, she walks out of the house... leaving me with this very emotional baby.

"What can I do to make you like me? Even just a little because this isn't working out." Maybe I have gone insane. I'm talking to a newborn like it's going to fix something. I decide to turn some music on so that I can have something to calm me down. I play some *Garth Brookes* on the house speaker and a miracle happens. She stops crying. I rock her while I sing along with the music and she falls asleep. Oh my shit. That's what she likes? I can sing country to her all day long if that's what it takes. I can't believe that's all it takes. I lay her down in her swing, buckle her in and walk away... very slowly. She stays asleep and I dramatically fall on the floor. I don't realize how long I stay in that position but when I hear the front door open, I assume it's been a while.

"Hey!" Ash screams over the music. It's not that loud and I swear if she wakes Ivy up, I will be pissed. She moves towards the controls and turns it down to where it's barley able to be heard. "Look at you. She's fast asleep. How does it feel?"

"It feels like I would love to hold my wife and take a nap." I wave her over to me.

"No sir, I will not be laying on the hard ass floor. But if you would like to lay on the couch, that can happen." She says and I stand, grunting the whole way up.

We snuggle up to each other with a blanket over us and just lay there. It's nice to have her in my arms like this, it's been a while. I kiss the top of her head and she pushes her face to my chest even more and I can feel her smile.

"This makes me happy. It's my kind of perfect." She says the same words that I did in the hospital and I smile.

Acknowledgments

Thank you so much for taking the time to read My Kind of Perfect, you are the real heroes.

This is a tiny one but I needed to write Jace as a dad and enjoyed every moment of it.

Of course, Ashley and Bethany... Y'all are amazing for sticking with me through all of this.

Thank you, my lovely arc readers.

About Author

S.L.Forrester is the author of Spice, Sass, and HEAs'. She lives in South Carolina with her husband and 3 kids. When she isn't writing, she's either dancing in her living room or reading. She listens to anything from country to 90s music and she reads fantasy and smut. Loads of smut. She cares for her friends like they are family.

If you want to follow her for future writings, look her up on Instagram, TikTok, Facebook, and Clapper at-

@S.L.Forrester

Also By

Taking The Shot
Yes Ma'am